A WERESHARK'S MEMOIR

A Wereshark's Memoir

JUSTIN T. O'CONOR SLOANE

Wild Man
of the
Woods
Press

ISBN: 979-8-9886342-8-7

Text © 2024 by Justin T. O'Conor Sloane

Editor & publisher, Justin T. O'Conor Sloane
Cover art: *Among the Waves* (1898)
by Ivan Konstantinovich Aivazovsky
Book design by Katerina von Brüno

Wild Man of the Woods Press
an imprint of
Starship Sloane Publishing Company, Inc.
Austin-Round Rock, Texas

starshipsloane.com

Justin Sloane's *A Wereshark's Memoir* is a true megalodon of a novelette, howling hammerheaded through the centuries, timeless like that eldest breed named for Greenland. Equal parts werewolf, shark, and swashbuckler who befriends Blackbeard himself, Sloane's narrator, sea-bewitched, bioluminescent shape-shifter, proves at least as haunted as a Ulysses unable ever to return home.

—Dr. Matt Schumacher, editor of *Phantom Drift: A Journal of New Fabulism* and author of *The Fire Diaries: Poems*

CONTENTS

Praise for A Wereshark's Memoir - v

~~

Preface
2

~~

A Wereshark's Memoir
5

About the Author - 42

PREFACE

It had been a while since I entertained my interest in the world of pirates, always a favorite subject of mine, so I sailed back into it with gusto! The surname Sloane (Ó Sluaghadháin) means "raider" in Gaelic, so maybe it's in the blood.

I was inspired to write this story when I learned that Richard Grieco was working on a new movie, *Time Pirates*, and that he was playing the fearsome pirate, Blackbeard. I've been a fan of Richard's acting since tuning in each week to watch *21 Jump Street*. Turns out that he's also a talented and accomplished visual artist. I've had the honor of publishing some of Richard's work over the years in various literary journals and magazines of Starship Sloane Publishing.

Interestingly enough, I once worked with a guy who claimed to be a descendant of Edward Thache Jr., better known as Edward "Blackbeard" Teach. I have no reason to doubt my colleague's claims of ancestry but for his exceptionally pacific disposition. Nevertheless, he was a fearless racecar driver and I think that must have been where he channeled his latent, piratical ferocity. I once went along for a ride with him on an improbably twisting road through the aspirationally nicknamed Issaquah Alps near Seattle and aged at least ten years during that infernal terror ride—one that would have made Blackbeard himself proud and would likely have flared his fuses into a full conflagration.

This novelette is the greatly expanded version of the short story that I originally wrote for the debut issue of *The Lotus Tree Literary Review*, winning first place in the 25th Annual Critters Readers' Poll in the science fiction & fantasy short story category.

I think that there is much more that could be written in this story as it follows a free flow of fantastical imagination and so there are really no limitations as to where it might ultimately make its journey, but I do consider it to be complete . . . at least for the time being.

Thank you for being here. I sincerely hope that you enjoy the story. Dive in for your richly deserved literary swim—but beware the odd wereshark lurking about.

Justin
November 2024
Deep in the heart of Texas, far from the sea.

~ 1 ~

A WERESHARK'S MEMOIR

I will say this before I begin in proper. My substance is best understood when measured in nautical miles of stealth and plunder. My history, the moon and the sea. My legend, a jewel of blood and saltwater.

This is my story.

I am a wereshark. We don't receive as much notice as our landlocked brethren. Granted, there are far more of them, we being a rarer breed indeed.

I have met only two others of my kind in all these centuries, not including young Teach in whose fate I played a role. Both far older than I and far more powerful. I was wise to stay a hemisphere away. They had progressed to a phantasmal state of bioluminescence when transformed. I found that to be most interesting. A menacing beauty. An expression of the moon and sea that wrought us.

My ancestors left Connacht in the west of Éire as the last of the high kings fell, the might of that ancient bloodline washing away with the rain into the moss and lichen, down through the rocks to the sea, as the storm and sword of a new and terrible history rolled dark

5

across that distant green altar, my Emerald Isle. For generations we roamed the coasts of the continent. Working as fishermen, seafarers, and shipwrights. A maritime legacy. I have never returned to the wild sea and green hills of Ireland. And I never will.

The sea has been my bright paradise, and it has been my darkest prison. It has been my joy, and it has been my torment. I have lived the sea like a salt-mad sailfish in the wind. To be a seaman, riding the currents, the winds, and the waves, has provided a measure of peace and camaraderie, grand adventure, and treasure beyond my most fevered dreams. It has also brought me notoriety—in which I once reveled. But to be a wereshark, in eternal bondage to the sea, has been a life unasked for.

Aqua. An axehard word for a substance soft and evaporative-ethereal. Terra firma. Ah, its peaceful sanctuary has done me much good, this recovering thalassophile.

Trees, now, my mast and sail, moss and lichen, my barnacled hull, fields of wind-driven grass, my green waves, meadows of wildflower abstraction, my coral reefs, still bogs, my saltwater lagoons, and always, the most delicious smell of rain.

Till the full moon calls me, as inescapably as it does the tides, to the sea.

The carnage, the sea-dog ferocity, the blood and saltwater, I am transmogrified, a shark and a man, with an almost human mind, but clouded, drugged, crazed, a thirst for blood of the sea drives me.

Once ashore, I go far from the seaside, deep into the mountains. A vegan with an almost hysterical aversion to seafood and any dish that once had blood. I say that I have allergies. I have become a solitary wanderer of forests and valleys, deserts and jungles. I follow legends and myths now, no longer the winds and currents of the Seven Seas. I search for the Seven Cities of Cibola and the many other lost cities of gold. I will find El Dorado one day, if it indeed exists. I search for the hoards of treasure cloaked in the mists of time. I search for the relics of rumor but find only whispers on the wind. I seek the unknown. The eternally hidden. The mysteries, the lore, the tales told around campfires and pints. I seek the lotus tree of Homer and Ovid. I have the time, so much time, and the blood-stained wealth to do as I wish. In truth, this is all just my entertainment, for I seek something else. Something greater, far greater. I traveled the Seven Seas long. Always looking for it. My crew as well, though they may not have realized. And I am still. That which sparkles and glitters, shining in a light all its own, far beyond any earthly riches. More splendid than all the treasure piled high and cascading of this material world. I didn't find it then. Though all of the many who were once my crew across the centuries, save Blackbeard, have. That I know. My command means nothing to them now. I am no longer their captain. The quick of sword and the bold of deed. They have another. But I seek it always. And I will never find it. This I also know. Such is the life of a wereshark. Such is not the life of a man or woman mere and mortal. Growing like wildflowers do, climbing their yellowshine trestle of sunlight into the blue and blossoming air, only to slowly fall, grayed and stooped with age, into the earth again. I live on.

I made my fortune long ago, aboard a swift ship of which I was the captain. Her name, the Ximena Feroz. A ship good and true. We were salt-flocked wolves of the sea, marauders drawn by mighty sails. The winds and the waves, leading us by their design, to each new opportunity in the glorious Age of Sail. There will never be another like it. Great sailing ships of discovery and commerce navigating the waters of the world. Sailing forth into the sun and the moon and the stars. Plying the known and charting the new. The future was ours. We would sail into it with sea salt in our beards and rum in our throats. A burning for treasure in our hearts. A most golden adventure it would be. The seagoing senses so alive. Salt air in the lungs and the symphony of wind on sail, mast, and wave. The fragrance of the sea, an elixir to the soul. The movement of wood on water, a meditation. The dance of wood and wave, a magic. The spray of the salted sea, a daily baptism. The compass rose and the mariner's astrolabe emblazoning my dreams. We sailed beneath the glory-bright heavens. We sailed on effervescence through the sparkling seas of crystalline sun showers. We sailed beneath skies of the highest blue and those that fluoresced green. We sailed above waters of the deepest blue and those that engulfed green. We saw things that could not be readily understood and others that gripped us by the back of the neck in the dead of night. We saw phantoms gliding at sea, spectral ships, strange lights and orbs floating about, and tiny phosphorescent water sprites dancing on the crests of waves. We heard the songs, weeping, and laughter of the sylphs, just at the edge of perception, murmuring on the winds and echoing in the sails. Women's voices gently called to us, rising from the troughs and from just beyond the swells. And at times, a tapping on the hull, that chilled us to the very marrow. Merfolk swam near the ship, vanishing as pale-green shadows beneath the surface. Creatures that shivered the timbers of our ship and great, barnacled tentacles that slapped the deck, and trailing seaweed, slid back into the depths. Coral reefs reflecting like great, bejeweled necklaces dropped by the sea giants of old. Storms that shook our bones and blinded our souls. Days that were but twilight. And seas that glowed blue at night. Whalesong, our strange lullaby from the deep.

Moments of high adventure that made me forget what I had become. Moments of riotous fun that shone bright the grand spectacle of life. An occasion found us surrounded by a roiling arribada of sea turtles so dense and vast that my landing party could not use the jolly boats, they hopped and reeled wildly across the great bubbling, carbonation of carapaces to the shore. I had nearly fainted with bullroar laughter. And there were moments of absolute tranquility. The embrace of a dense fog on a serene sea was to ascend into the silent, white cathedral of the clouds themselves. And the sea was my cathedral. It was my worship. And it was my captor.

We once came upon a long-dead man crucified in the Roman fashion, a near-skeletal vision of a Christ at sea, the cross affixed to a great log raft. He rode the waves like a grinning scarecrow, disappearing into the troughs and leaping out at us atop his cresting craft, as though playing a sinister game of peekaboo. Those of my men who still felt the weight of religion on their soul, muttered prayers to the Redeemer and trembling, made the sign of the cross. At my hoarse command, we grappled his craft to ours, poured lamp oil over the side and sent him off as a torch aflame. It was then I first took notice that the spars of my ship formed crosses, and I, in my darkest, most fiendish hours of sea-wrought madness, had men nailed high about, leaving them to return in bits to the deck below. Though my most inspired was to become known as the Devil's Shish Kabob. I will provide no details here. Whether such wickedness was born of my own heart or of the unholy abomination I had been made into, I do not rightly know.

By the Golden Age of Piracy, I had long since become a legend of the high seas. When in battle, it was said that my face blazed as fire, that I moved as a quick flame, consuming all before me. I was called Captain of the Wine-Red Hand. And at times, simply, the Red Captain. My emerald-hilted cutlass was whispered of from the Bosporus Strait to the Indian Ocean. It was boasted that using just one of the Apostles from around my waist, I could both shave the skinny whiskers off a man at spyglass distance with my pistol and fillet a flying fish right into the galley cook's pan. I was that very seaborne plague that begat a perpetual fear. The Jolly Roger, as it came to be known by the bastard English, was the rum-soaked work of my own artistic hand and to none we met, jolly. I was no Mither o' the Sea. My men knew hard well that when the full moon rose, safety could only be found far aloft in the rigging, the nearer to St. Elmo's Fire the better, he, the patron saint of sailors. On more than one occasion, a lad of my crew had slipped from the yards, plummeting like a diving seabird, at the sight of my moonlit form. My agelessness was a subject of suspicious wonder and mystery to all who did not know my true nature. Mariners told the tale that under a red sky at morning, I had gained immortality by offering a ship laden with fleur de sel, its sails washed burgundy with the blood of my foes, to the crimson-embered devil himself. And that soon thereafter, a screaming tempest had brought a red and boiling, sulfurous sea. Steam and vapor rose high, and "AYE" was writ large in the foul air for all to see. The bargain had been accepted. The contract signed in brimstone and saltwater, as it were. My eternal youth and the exploits attributed to me were taken as incontrovertible proof of that most vile transaction.

I have been called a privateer, a corsair, a buccaneer, a freebooter, and a pirate—depending on time and place and occasional employ. I have been called the Saltwater Devil, the Devil's Own Squall, and even the Devil of the

Sea. In fact, I have been called everything but a child of God. Verily, multitudes were the ship that found itself between the devil and the deep blue sea as my dread crew and I drew nigh. I have made many the man, good and bad alike, walk the plank and I have keelhauled many more. I was no pleasantry then as now. I have taught a legion of riches-hungry souls the ways of a plundering life at sea down through the ages. Young Teach, who came to braid fuses into his black beard, got his start under my command and owes me his life, then and still. My ship was never lost, never captured, but freely given upon my departure from the daily sea.

It is a quiet life for me now. And secretive, as it has long been. Red wine and rum, too much, and poetry, too little. An earnest splash of paint here and there. Reminding me that I'm no Pollack. Some classical music, a new pleasure in the days of yore. I once ordered my men to capture a squeaking man and his gleaming harpsichord. We lashed them securely to the foremast and had the music of a palace court at sea for a time. But full moon comes calling, a sinister carnival barker levitating bright aglow. I plan ahead, renting Lambos and Ducatis, flooring them to the coast. This fish-to-be can drive like Mario Andretti—and ride a bike, too. Diving deep from cliff tops, displaying expert technique, a lycanthropene Greg Louganis. I'm more dorsal fin than man by three strokes in. Neptune deliver whatever I might find down there. I once catapulted myself upon a scuba club on their annual full-moon dive—a fundraising event for endangered sea turtles. One of their imprinted snorkels washed ashore in Fiji five years later, cocooned in sea life, and made the international news. A flipper, bite mark and all, had been found in a tide pool halfway to Santa Monica and a chewed-up diving suit-come-suborbital-projectile, gyrating as a windsock from a coastal cypress one county over. It was as though a crate of toothy TNT had detonated right in the middle of their little soirée in the sea. I can't help but chuckle. Many the surfer has escaped my terrible jaws as I laughed uncontrollably beneath the waves, green-eyed tears to the sea, watching them paddle furiously in a swell of profound and pissing terror. I don't feel guilty anymore. I do what I am. I didn't ask to become this cursed creature of the fathomless marine, those many centuries long ago, along that moonlit Sicilian coastline.

It was my honeymoon and my last moments as a mortal man. Memories of my sweet wife haunt me still. I walked on the beach as she slept, her long black hair flowing from the bed, swaying gently as kelp in the sea breeze. I had gazed out upon the shimmering, hypnotic expanse of the night sea from our balcony. Felt the gravity of the heavy moon pulling at my blood and was drawn to the surf in a swoon. Each receding wave calling me closer. I enjoyed the feel of cool sand between my toes and the lapping of seawater at my ankles. The sweeping flash and long eclipse of a far distant lighthouse spoke a peculiar mixture of comfort and solitude as I walked luxuriously in the ancient histories of Mediterranean civilization. It's sunken ships, battles between warring empires on the sea, and explorers sailing forth to shape destiny enveloped me as fully as any sea mist would. The full moon, that most radiant goddess, or so I once thought of her, watered my eyes, so low I could have reached out for a pinch of moon dust. I drank cognac from the bottle my wife and I had bought in Corsica and reveled in my joy on that splendid shoreline. Smoking Spanish tobacco long in transit, the fragrance of a new world, I had been making bold and daring plans for a seafaring future. Horror sometimes finds you when you least expect it, and least deserve it. I never saw her again, my raven-haired wife, but it is just as well. For I am a demon. Moon spawn of sea foam and dark waves. A pale demon of the deep blue sea. What other am I? And she, a saint. A saint of the calm depths, the currents, and the churning whitecaps. My patroness saint, Saint of the Seven Seas. The keeper of a sacred ember of light in the distant altar of my mind. The saint of my most hallowed memories.

And so it is. A solitary life. Forlorn even.

And I have searched . . . relentlessly . . . for any information that I can find concerning my wife. Our honeymoon cut short by the cruel timing of my transformation on that moonlit Sicilian shore so long ago. I employ historians to scour archival records abroad, but have yet to find anything but the pale dust of old sorrows. It is a void in my soul. Through which a cold and screaming wind blows. This is all I will say in the matter.

But what of Blackbeard you may ask? He pays me a visit from time to time. He is the respected captain of a merchant ship now. His pirating history has been very well chronicled, but his current identity is unknown. Great wealth can buy almost anything, in his case, a new life. One with the respect of society and with professional dignity. He's become a devout Christian. One would never know now the terrors he once wrought. Like rain on a roof, it has flowed away, been absorbed and obscured, and become something new. New life. Like leaves sprouting from branches. I am happy for him. He, as I, had not asked for this fate. He, as I, was not deserving of this fate. But, in the grand scheme of things, deserving and receiving are two entirely unrelated things. I know that now. As does he. As the days of pirating—at least as we knew them to be—came to an end, we had agreed to scuttle the Ximena Feroz, that finest of ships, rather than let any other use her for anything other than what had long been her destiny proud, that of a feared and magnificent pirating ship of such superb elegance and trusted seaworthiness that she had won a fame unknown to any other sailing ship. It took me many long years to finally dry my tears. Blackbeard, too. We loved that fierce ship like life itself. As it sank beneath the waves, so too, sank our hearts, and when it vanished from view, so too, the lives we had known. Forevermore. It was then a time of reinvention for Blackbeard. The time had come for him to begin writing a new chapter in his life's story. I was already writing mine. But when our ship no longer sailed the seas, resting beneath, so too the inklines of destiny dried in their clear finality. Forward. Only forward. Our past lies beneath the bluegreen waves of the sea.

I have removed myself from the tyranny of daily chores and mundane concerns. I hire many to do much. I have also endeavored to extricate myself from social obligations and interactions to the greatest extent possible. I desire neither society nor what it offers, beyond its ability to support the freedoms of my lifestyle.

I once trekked north to revel in the aurora borealis. Commissioning a pilot, I dropped from on high in a glider, sailing silently through the swirling green spectacle spilling about the atmosphere like great rivers of light flowing from the heavens. This reminded me greatly of my days at sea. It brought me that same sense of expansive joy and adventure, but as it was not the sea, I did not feel bound to it. It was an exhilarating freedom that I experienced in those precious moments.

In much the same way, I surfed the great beams of light of a full moon as they broke in silverbright waves through the anthracite clouds, finally transmogrifying in view of the white caps below. My timing was very well executed. I ditched the glider in a controlled frenzy and dove deep into the intoxicating Pacific, a dark and dazzling pool of undulating moonshine.

I have battled the giant Pacific octopus in the cold, dark depths of Puget Sound, their skin a raging red and have given orcas far more than they bargained for. Great whites see me as their own and so I have not yet had the pleasure of combat with their ilk.

I have noticed that I too, have begun to luminesce, just as I had seen the other two of my kind do, they far older and more powerful than I. I will someday terminate their hemispheric reign. The same may come to pass one day with Blackbeard, but I would prefer to think that we should remain friends. There need not be only one.

I have endeavored with the ironmost will of discipline for centuries now to develop the powers of telekinesis. My thinking in the matter is that with enough time and focused meditation, plumbing the greatest depths of the mind and exploring its most remote and uncharted properties and potential, that I should be able to achieve this objective, that I should be able to manifest this power if it is indeed possible, as some would suggest. I have not yet succeeded. But I will not let my disappointment in this practice dissuade me from continuing to try.

I do notice though that I have an exceptionally heightened sense of perception, I would venture to say that it borders on being ESP, or that it may even be ESP. This is an exciting possibility to me, but I cannot yet differentiate between the possibility that it is the heightened senses of a shark driving this ability or if it originates independently. Time, meditation, and deeply intuitive processes of the mind will eventually lead me to the answers I seek.

As an entertainment, I purchased a balloon capable of reaching the stratosphere. I had seen a Swiss man by the name of Piccard do just such a thing. It inspired me and focused my energies externally for a time. I trained in its piloting and set off to enjoy this newfound and grand sport. I had been impatient in my learning and training and had made many errors in calculation, including that of duration. I had not even bothered to hire a ground control, thinking that my experience as a captain in great gails and typhoons would have prepared me for anything. A balloon is not a sailed ship and my conceits in the matter faded as quickly as the ground beneath me. I was not as good with the instrumentation as I should have been. I would soon learn the error of my ways. A lesson in humility and baffled helplessness that I required but once to become a much wiser being. Forethought and careful preparation are the keys to success in any endeavor, of which I was pointedly reminded. As I gained great elevation events began to unfold in a decidedly contrary fashion to what I had planned and I was not able to descend. To begin with, the winds of the upper atmosphere behave far differently than the saltwater-kissed winds of the sea. They are also as cold as any cube of ice. And they never subside. Drawing you along streams of air that circle the globe. Much time passed. Then much more. As I drifted over the western Pacific Ocean one night I was shocked to see the full moon present itself mightily. I had been high adrift for many days and had paid no attention to the phases of the moon, being so utterly immersed in the details of my instrumentation and attempting to overcome my deficit of training in piloting a high-altitude balloon. I felt the frenzy come upon me. It seemed more powerful than usual, perhaps being closer to the moon energized the transformation in a way that I had not yet experienced. The frenzy soon hit such a fevered pitch that I had lost all sense of reason. Beyond that, the change was happening far more quickly and the need to be in saltwater became more urgent than it had ever been before. Unable to descend, traveling at a tremendous speed through the frigid sky, inexorably transforming within the gondola, I became a berserker, tearing the cockpit to pieces and ripping the entry portal from its hinges. A split second later, I was free falling through the atmosphere, plummeting towards the ocean at such an extreme velocity that I was reintroduced to a long-forgotten emotion: fear. A giddying and unrelenting fear that soon evaporated into a kind of strange euphoria. I did not know if I could survive such a fall, even when fully transformed, which I now was. But I knew that I needed to knife into the water if I were to have any chance at all. Through a series of furious contortions and maneuvers I managed to align myself as a diver would, entering the water moments later with a cracking boom. My body, violently shuddered by the slicing impact, stung as though engulfed by 10,000 hornets. I blacked out a moment later. How long I was unconscious I do not know. But when I awoke I knew myself to be many leagues deeper than I had ever been. I could feel a great pressure surrounding me, pushing in on me, unlike anything I had previously experienced. I was slowly drifting deeper, in a gentle swaying motion like that of a hammock, looking up through the black of the water, my eyes unable to focus on anything. I felt a sudden surge of claustrophobia shimmer through my being and a strobing confusion; both of these were also alien and long forgotten sensations. I knew that I needed to take action and begin swimming to regain my sense of equilibrium and agency. I shot upwards with a white-hot and blazing fury of purpose. Soon, light began to diffuse the water as the surface drew nearer. I relaxed my efforts and began zigzagging horizontally in a leisurely fashion. In command of my senses once more and feeling like any other shark of the sea again, I smiled a toothy grin through the dark-green water and set off to pursue lunch. Later, calculating my estimated velocity, the coefficient of friction, and the density of water, among other factors, I came to understand that I had managed to thread the needle and plunge many leagues deep into the Mariana Trench itself. I have not gone near a balloon of any size since.

Through devices of the most exquisite cunning and subterfuge, I have managed to lure werewolves to the shores of the sea, whereupon, I have pulled them beneath the surf in a flash and ripped them asunder. Paying no heed to what they may have been in their daily lives. If they were accountants in the light of the sun, then ledgers will go untabulated. And thus it will be. The were-life is a dangerous one indeed and I have a deep and abiding hatred for those hairy, howling beasts. As I have stated, I am no pleasantry.

My memories besiege me, yet they are all that I have really. They define me.

Once, while floating the windless, infinite blues and browns of the Sargasso Sea, a great glowing craft descended silently from the starbright heavens and took a deckhand away with it through a strange apparatus of silver light, up through which the poor lad rose against his best efforts, Newton's apple but contrary to the intentions of nature. We fired our pistols at the craft as it tarried about our masts and managed a volley from the cannons as it flew slowly around us in an ever-widening circle, then flashed from sight at a speed the likes of which we had no ken and that left our eyes moist with the dew of a sober disbelief and our faces irrigated by the anxious rivulets of water that flowed freely from our brows. I quickly decided upon the appropriate course of action to find our pirating bearings, grog be damned, I ordered fresh barrels of rum brought topside from the spirit room and we drank for hours upon end, singing rowdy songs til every man jack stumbled to his hammock below decks or slid to his boots and slept in the velvety seabreeze of sugarcane fields distilled into firenectar on the not distant islands of the Caribbean.

Moving through swaying kelp forests, made aglow with shafts of moonlight, an illumination of ethereal green, I find tranquility within my animal self for some brief moments at a time. But like a racehorse out of the gates, I'm soon rushing forward to seek new carnage.

When I think of what the ocean has consumed and created through its systems of digestion and renewal through the many millions of years, I know myself to be as inconsequential as any grain of sand on its shores. A cosmos of sand reflected within a cosmos of stars. But, this I also know. That I must therefore make my own meaning, through the consequence of my mind, ideas and personal philosophy manifested through the action of my hands into a physical reality. This is what my God requires of me. It is not the God of the many, it is my God. My God alone. No explanation necessary, no converts desired, no like-minded connections with others sought. I am a wereshark. Few of us exist, no two really alike. No mortal capable of meeting us where we are. And so. And so, I am the sum total of the spirituality of my own God. I am the past, the present, and the future. I am the chosen one. I am the disciple. It serves me well.

I enter the great Christian cathedrals from time to time. To try to feel that expression of the divine. It does not supplant my God. I had once thought myself beyond the shadow of religion, yet I have become my own religion. A strange irony, I suppose.

The Galápagos Islands, were to me the most enchanted of archipelagos. The Enchanted Isles. More so than any other. The Tortoise Islands, their very name. I saw in their volcanic proclamation the very processes whereby life migrated from the sea to the land. A severity of rock and a profusion of unique creatures that I had not glimpsed elsewhere. Giant tortoises like ambling, green haystacks and enormous, black lizards with vibrant, green patches that swam and dove beneath the waves and those that were of the brightest citrus yellows and oranges, while others still, were a hellish pink, scrambling across a primordial landscape hot as the devil's own soul. And boobies, but with bright blue feet, as though dipped in the finest of artists' paint. And none had a fear of man in them. A source of their demise. We cooked tortoises in the great cauldron of their own shell over bonfires aflash with spilled rum and fanciful tales and celebrated our hardy-good fortune. We provisioned great quantities of fresh water, a marvel that such could be found on these grand rocks jutting from the Pacific. Floreana Island was a favorite spot, a cave in Asilo de la Paz provided respite from the sun and located nearby, a freshwater spring quenched our thirst as no bottle of rum or cup of grog could. The many splendid coves sheltered my beloved ship and I put these islands on our map as a refuge to revisit. A pirate's paradise.

Humans in submersibles are a particular delight for me. I toy with them, terrorizing them, before sending them to rest forevermore in Davey Jones' Locker. He, the true devil of the sea, not I, though I have been called that at times—and deservedly so—while still a captain of the high seas.

I had heard the tales of a red shadow. And I have seen it, this entity, while swimming the coastal inlets of the Pacific, shores engulfed by wildfires that clawed as red fingers, like lava flows, at the slopes of distant mountains. A vaporous figure, barely discernible, scintillating the colors of fire, moving slowly among the towering torches, a great cloak of trailing flame. Stopping to admire the most radiant of embers, as one would wildflowers. And standing, arms outstretched, within a wall of thundering flame, as though it were a waterfall.

Time is a funny thing. And I have much time. Time to think. Too much thinking. And the more I think, the less anything really makes any sense to me. When I concentrate on a word long enough, saying it over and over, it begins to lose all meaning. It does not gain more. I do not gain some special insight. Rather, it simply becomes nonsense. I often wonder why that is. Why is meaning ephemeral? That to concentrate on meaning, it dissipates, like a sea fog before the sun? But I have learned. I know now. Meaning is what you make it. And what you make of it.

I have seen the apparitions of drowned sailors a league deep in the open ocean. They move along the currents, like jellyfish, translucent and hollowed out. Drifting. An obscured evaporation of life, grainy recordings seen through a mist ringing the eyes. Their netherworld interfaces with ours. I have no answer to their mystery.

I have spent time in the Devil's Triangle. Bermuda holds many fond memories for me. Barrels of rum and more booty than one can easily imagine. I have found no indication of paranormal activity, neither then nor now. However, strange occurrences abound there. I have first-hand experience. I think it to be strange natural energies from the planet itself. Electromagnetic fields that wreak havoc on a ship's instrumentation and cause various hallucinations through its action upon the human mind. Modern science, in which I hold much faith, shows this to be so in connection with such. I vastly enjoy a good ghost story, but I can ascribe none to this very odd place. Though I would heartily like to do so.

I have, however, found what I believe to be the sunken city of Atlantis. I seek still the remnants of the lost continent of Lemuria, an irrational search for it is a discredited theory. I have found evidence of other great civilizations, rivaling Atlantis, neither conjectured of nor even hinted at by mankind. Civilizations that long preceded our own and have been obliterated by the ravages of time. I have found technologies long since ensconced in sedimentary rock that speak to these previous iterations of highly advanced human civilizations. I can only surmise as to the great calamities that brought about their downfall.

Most astonishingly, I once discovered an alien ship, contained as though it were a fly in amber, at the bottommost extent of a glacier still graduating its way into the Southern Ocean, beneath which I swam. The salt water had polished the ice, creating a lens of sorts through which to view the artifact. It looked as though it were made of quicksilver. It was just beyond my ability to see its details clearly, though its shape was unmistakable. A saucer-like ship, similar to the other, reflecting a silver sheen through a great frozen veil. It raised many questions and disquieted my closest held sense of history. Intent upon documenting my discovery, I had returned, but the ship was gone, its coffin of ice having been torn asunder by the sea.

I have gathered, like the mysterious Captain Nemo, great quantities of bullion from the wrecks of Spanish galleons. For I can go where none are easily able, unhindered by ordinary constraints. I have found some by chance, some by memory, and some through careful research and expedition. I have meditated upon the good that gold can do. And the evil. It is an otherworldly substance, its properties unique and its value comprehended as being more than that assigned to it by man. It has a preternatural beauty. Sunshine. In solid form. Sunlight. Made tangible. The product of a strange and cosmic alchemy. One that exerts an influence over our minds that goes beyond the fevered lust that it incites in us for the extravagances of wealth that it permits. Rather, its power lies in the world of our dreams. Dreams caught. Dreams woven. Dreams made. Gold the dream maker. The dream manifester. My vast riches are regularly supplemented by this most enjoyable of hobbies—the retrieval of bullion long lost. It is a tranquility.

I have felt the remote age of the universe in the wind, sensed its steady expansion like the turning hands of a clock, felt its limitless and alien expanse in the warmth of the sun, sensed the flashing temporality of life in the rocky geology upon which I stood. The feeling was that of an endless plain in the gloaming. Millennia falling away like the petals of an old flower.

I have heard the susurrus of high-energy particles torrenting through the atmosphere. Have felt the atoms dancing on my skin, detected them teeming in the air about me, an evaporative and all-encompassing cloud of specks moving just beyond routine perception. We are awash in atoms. A cosmic ocean of atoms from which a cohort is drawn together into a discrete form, traveling a unique energy pathway for the briefest moment in time, then dispersing, flowing back into the ocean atomic, star travelers, flotsam among the galaxies.

A physical universe is a stark place. Cold to the soul. The only insulation being the beliefs in which we wrap ourselves. In these moments I have felt a sense of profound isolation. And sadness. Maybe that will change, but I did not feel a sense of tranquility and oneness. I did not feel a sense of spirituality connecting me to some grand and purposeful cosmic architecture of harmonic energies and celestial vibrations. I just felt strange, an incoherence of being, empty inside. A hollow kite far aloft, through which the ceaseless winds of time blew.

This opening up to the infinite and indifferent scale of the universe has not been the catalyst for some great spiritual epiphany. Rather, it has been dismal. And deeply unsettling. It is only something that I have experienced because I have time, so much time. It was not precipitated by mindfulness or meditation, just idle time. In the frenetic dealings of a mortal life, one has so little time.

The mad race consumes us, our every waking moment, and jars us from the sanctuary of our slumber.

The sound of the sea was almost soothing in these moments. These moods. And I often went to it. But it fell short of being so. For it was also hollow. A sound disconnected and untethered. Scattered frequencies tumbling through the wind. And I felt separate from it, removed, perhaps even a sense of having turned away, a cherished and long distant home that I could never return to in innocence.

I think that I now better understand why mortals cling to one another pathologically, madly, feverishly, why they numb their senses with intoxicants and cloud themselves with mindless entertainment. It is an illusion of solace. And they feel it to be so. It is flimsy, false, and fleeting. An artifice. If you aren't at peace with your place in the universe and with what the universe is, then there is no solace to be had. Maybe that's the spiritual part, I don't know. I don't pretend to know. I'll leave that to the charlatans. And to those very few who actually do.

Madness comes easily enough. Washing over me like the waves of the North Sea. But I regain my buoyancy, always through sheer force of will, the blazing light of which drives the deep and ever-grasping shadows to a thwarted distance. Though my dark transformation brought about many things, an immunity of the psyche and of the soul was not one of them. Even I, the Captain General of the Sea—il Capitano Generale da Mar, was not invulnerable to the tempests of my own nature. But given enough time and singular focus, perhaps I could become so. And perhaps, perhaps God will present itself in a form that I can recognize. For I know it to be possible that what I have just described to you is in fact God presenting itself to me. Who am I to impose my expectations on that experience?

And so. Experiences. At times, I reflect upon my condition and gain some measure of appreciation for the experiences it allows me. Experiences far beyond the ken of mortals. The thresholds of the physical being do not limit me in comparison. I am able to comfortably withstand what would surely kill mortals in an instant. Nor am I limited by a need for sleep. And though I hunger and thirst, it is more driven by a desire and an instinct to kill than by the actual need for nourishment to sustain my physical being and my efforts. But that is while the moon is full. My weakness besets me before and after my three days of havoc are wreaked upon the world each month, for that is when I become almost like you. Almost mortal. It is when I am weak that I wish to be something other than I am. But during the glorious hysteria of my transformation, I revel in my powers. Which have heightened greatly since my inception. And they will continue to. I am most curious to see the extent to which they do. And as mentioned, I relish the thought of vanquishing my older colleagues who share in this condition. I feel this way even when not in a state of transformation. Mayhap I have always had a twist of the evil in me. Perhaps this is why I was chosen. Or I have become so. I do not rightly know. My long meditations on this matter over the years have led me no closer to the truth of my spiritual substance than I was five-hundred years ago. Knowledge of my true being is an elusive and hard sought prize. I had journeyed to Nepal, and later Tibet, hoping to find my truth of essence through the isolation of Buddhist practice. I envisioned finding enlightenment in a monastery high in the Himalayas. But the distance from the sea soon proved a profound impracticality and I have not returned since. I had endeavored to bring a monk to California to further my practice in meditation, but word of what I was had spread, seemingly telepathically, among the communities there and none would accept my proposition. I would not hire any but them. And so it is. Even the greatest of wealth cannot buy everything as it turns out. Interesting—and as it should be—that it is in the realm of the spiritual that the buck does indeed stop. Crooked pastors notwithstanding.

I have pushed myself to the extreme, to the very limits in my transformation and managed to swim further and faster than I had ever imagined possible. Always at the back of mind is that I might encounter one of the elders. It will happen eventually. I have rehearsed time and again my actions in that situation. A bold and decisive attack is the best strategy and the only real option. I push myself to quicken the process of my strengthening. I have noticed that while maturation through age amplifies and grows my powers, so too does the physical stress with which I subject myself. I am in training therefore, to dispose of those whom I know would wish to do the same with me—and think nothing of it. Long ago, I had met my elders by chance, one soon after the other as fate would have it. I escaped with my life but only narrowly. Elements had been in my favor both times, an advantage that allowed for the slimmest margins of escape. Their power was formidable, but I also sensed that neither would have been my match before our respective inception. This translation of both natural and battle-won abilities helped my cause in those moments, if only slightly. My survival was measured in milliseconds and millimeters. I swore that upon our next meeting, the tables would be reversed and victory would be mine. I have since escalated my aspiration from that of mere victory to their demise. I will not look over my shoulder for a thousand years. Then another. I will not fear the attack of a most dangerous and sophisticated enemy. Rather, it will be I who attacks. If by ambush, sobeit. I have focused my mind on this course of action and my resolve in the matter has crystallized. Forming a geological intent. The accretion of my thoughts as real as any stone dagger in the hand, chiseled by time, burnished with anticipation and fired hard and sinister by a dark desire. I will have my blood.

Only the creatures of the great marine know that sunlight will make two parts of the same sea a blue and a green and when they mix, a kaleidoscope of color bursts forth beneath the waves. I have seen saltwater sizzle with golden sheets of sunlight, effervescing yellow bubbles into a bluebright, refracting air. I stay as deep as necessary to avoid direct contact with sunlight, but although such would be painful, it would not be deadly for me. I am, after all, no vampire. And make no mistake, there are vampires of the sea. I have beheld them. They live in the wreckage of sunken ships and prey on scuba divers and cruise ship passengers. They are an especially unpleasant lot and prone to cruel fits of a waterborne melancholy, lamenting a long distant and preferred life on land. I have not yet been able to ascertain how they found themselves to be in their present circumstances. They are most unfriendly and not at all receptive to conversation. And so, I can only conjecture. Another mystery for my book of mysteries. It has been said that the great underwater explorer Jacques Cousteau once encountered members of this disagreeable race, retiring soon thereafter. I know not if there is any truth to the story.

I have often pursued my fascination with the bizarre realm of fungi. The Roman god of fungi, Robigus, was greatly revered and feared. And most rightly so. That a mushroom is the flower of a fungus residing deep beneath the surface of the soil, sending up a long filament to the light, that they are classified as being neither plant nor animal, has sparked a great and enduring curiosity within me. They possess a chemical intelligence, a chemical communication transmitted through vast, subterranean territories. A deep kingdom of the darkest chambers. A labyrinth of fungal intelligence. Fungi can make zombies of wasps and other creatures, controlling their very behavior. They are a strange and alien life form. Look no further for otherworldly intelligences, we share our own with many. I have wondered if perhaps a luciferin and luciferase producing fungus or alga is the reason for the ever-intensifying bioluminescence of my race? (Ah! There he is again. Lucifer. The light-bringer.) Alga means seaweed in Latin, and I am brought back to the sea, always back to the sea. I once dug down 35 feet below the forest floor in the wilderness of Oregon to get at the fungus from which the mushroom flowered. I sensed it to be hostile to my efforts, like unearthing some pale and dangerous insect just beneath the soil of a rock, a presence better left hidden by its own dark devices. A gray and misshapen, fleshy mass, insinuated throughout the soil, an alien brain, pulsing malevolence. I smelled its sinister intelligence, a chemical signature that left my heightened olfactory sense smarting for days after. I have done battle with the hissing Yateveo plant of South America, the Devil's Snare of Central America and the Madagascar tree among others, but while their aggression was of a seemingly automatic and purely physical nature, like that of the Venus flytrap, this presented an insidious and pervading atmosphere of hostile intent. A telepathic malice manifested by a keen and formidable intelligence. Perhaps the product of the combined forces of fungal networks and colonies that stretch for miles, silent and mostly unseen, deep below our feet, as has been found. I cannot be entirely sure if the organism was inherently evil, or simply employing a strategy of deterrence—ultimately justified, though I meant it no real harm—intended to thwart the invasion of its underground domain. I am, however, inclined to believe the former. That fungi do not rely upon chlorophyl to conduct photosynthesis for survival leads me to question their origins. That various mushrooms also contain powerful hallucinogens and poisons has further fueled my curiosity concerning this strange life form. They are able to manipulate our perceptions and to kill. They are chemists. Dependent upon neither the light of the sun nor moonglow. I no longer consume mushrooms. Perhaps there will come a day when there will be more things in this world that I avoid than those that I do not. Only time will tell.

As I have told you, in my human form, I eschew all forms of meat, whether from on land or from in sea. I had begun as a vegan, but unable to abstain from enjoying the many delights of dairy I am now simply a vegetarian, but that is the extent of my direct culinary interaction with animal products. I have at times bought out the entirety of the lobsters crawling about restaurant aquariums, rubber bands on their claws, to release them into the sea. This amuses me. I am perhaps the patron saint of the lobster. A strange creature that is quite delicious despite some of its more unsavory insectoid aspects. I have consumed many the line of marching lobsters during my time in transformation, my jaws appreciating the exercise, like chewing gum when I am bored during my dry-land sojourns. But when human, I am repulsed by the idea of consuming creatures of the sea and land. A surf and turf restaurant is the most abhorrent of places to me now. Long before all of this though, I loved such eateries. In Italy, I recall a little cafe near Rome, but closer to the sea, that served an exquisite crab carbonara. I shudder now to think of the dish. Frustrated with the readily available and mass-produced offerings for vegetarians, I invested in creating my own line of ready-made, vegetarian cuisine. I am very happy with it and it is selling very well. Wealth begets more wealth, but I donate all profits to charitable organizations, à la Newman's Own, especially those that protect the sea from the ravages of human civilization.

I once desired a career in film. I had the time. Why not the fame and the lark? I laugh now. What a repugnant and odious industry. Hedonistic hypocrites of the highest order. Miscreants, perverts, and drug addled ne'er do wells who desperately crave the attention of others. Pathetic. I soon learned the error of that ambition. I am many things, but I am not suited to the life of an actor. In my days at sea I would have run such unholy fiends through with my cutlass. The Romans buried actors in separate cemeteries, no sign of respect and a sensibility that I now understand fully. And I have done long and frequent battle with Roman galleys and hold nothing but the utmost respect for that great and warring race of man. If not a Hibernian, I would have most desired to be a Roman.

I thirst for the most dire of consequences for aberrant behavior. In my time as a sea captain, absolute order was upheld through the gravest of punishments. Though I were a pirate, aboard my ship, absolute order ruled. The rule of my law was absolute. One knew what one would get if the rules were broken, if our code of conduct was not adhered to. All were content as all knew the consequences for their actions. No leniency was given. No excuses accepted. No justifications made. No exploitations of loopholes. There was no agenda but quick justice. I see a society now that would benefit from the same enforcement of laws as that aboard a pirate ship. I see endless excuses and finger pointing, deflection and redirection, a lack of personal responsibility, justifications, rationalizations, misguided appeasement and the enabling of more of the same. I see relativistic arguments and worldviews, such that truth, standards and the norms of human conduct will eventually cease to exist. I see an erosion in values and ethics and a wholesale destruction of the collective moral compass. I see the criminal painted as the victim and the victim stripped of their justice. None of that would be allowed on a pirate ship. Consequences are meted out for actions done. Period. Are you surprised to hear a once-feared pirate speak like this? You shouldn't be. We may have been wolves of the high sea, but we abided strictly by a code of conduct that was enforced with ruthless and lethal efficiency. An eye for an eye leaves the whole world blind some would say. What utter rubbish I say! If the actions warrant it, sobeit, for without it, an attitude of indifference and disobedience develops, creeping in bit by bit like a vile mold and eventually devouring law and order, putrefying it, hollowing it out and rendering it worthless. Replacing consequences for one's actions with falsities, warped platitudes, disingenuous apologies, and no actual contrition is the road to society's ruin, just as it would be on any pirate ship of old. There was a time that a thief's hand was cut off for stealing. Now the thief is made to be the victim and the baker the criminal. Nothing works better to keep the human animal in line than fear and retribution. On my ship, fear made my men lawful. Lawlessness was not given the chance to fester. It was stamped out like a hissing cockroach. As such, we were highly efficient in our endeavors for no clouds of doubt hung about the ship. No gray. Just black and white. Much like the Jolly Roger itself. I hold to the severest of punishments and discipline for those who choose to break the laws. It has served me well and I would have it no other way. Society would do well to adopt the same approach. But I am not a man of this day and age. And so, I remain baffled. But what of my own great lawlessness, you may ask? Aye, if I were to have been caught, I would have accepted my fate and the consequences of my deeds. I would not have asked for forgiveness nor lenience. I would not have blamed my transformation. I chose my path of blood and plunder—no other.

When I am deep in my cups and memories flow like wine from my mind to my heart as from the bottle to the chalice, I feel again the embrace of my wife, though centuries removed, as if it were only moments ago. Time is a fleeting stag, a blurred and distant vapor before unfocused eyes. Time is neither friend nor foe. But it can be made either. It is of your choosing. I once made it my enemy. But no longer. And time has forgiven me my foolishness. It is the only friend I have now, save Blackbeard.

Ah, Blackbeard. I think him to be a loyal friend but I cannot be sure. Perhaps he entertains the same notions towards me that I entertain towards the elder ones. Perhaps he harbors a thousand, clawing hatreds of me for changing him. It takes years long to come to terms with one's transformation into a wereshark. Perhaps someday he will attempt my assassination. And perhaps he will prevail. Until then, we shall drink together as only sailors of the high seas can, pirates we, those who have done many a long battle shoulder to bloody shoulder, back to bloody back.

And here we come to the part of my memoir that is most unexpected. It was for me the equivalent of wandering out of Plato's cave and seeing the world for what it really was. No more shadows. I had always believed that my transformation had been wrought by a confluence of natural elements and strange energies on the night of my change on that serene beach in Sicily. Some strange alchemy. An interaction born of pure and extraordinary chance. I remembered nothing of it and as I awoke on the shores of a distant land, profoundly confused but otherwise unscathed, and as I did not yet understand what I had become, the thought that a creature of the night sea and the full moon had done this to me had not entered my mind. Not then, and not even much later. Rather, the truth was delivered to me as lightning in the night.

You can imagine my surprise when I learned the truth. The truth of my origin. Read on, sweet soul, as my life's tale nears its completion to the here and now.

There is a third elder. The one that changed me. I did not learn of her existence until quite recently. Her age and power are beyond reckoning. I would stand no chance in battle against her, but neither do I desire to do so. I met her in the open ocean, somewhere between Madagascar and Australia. It was not a chance encounter. She had finally decided to introduce herself to me. Perhaps judging me to be ready for such, to have matured. My anguishes blunted by time. And she was kind. Benevolent. It was most unexpected. The others I had met were instantly hostile, cruel and aggressive, intent upon killing me. This elder was almost motherly. She has progressed to a permanent state of transformation, unaffected by the full moon, the light of the sun, saltwater or freshwater, or even the need for carnage. She lives as any shark might. No more, no less, really, but for the exceptional intelligence of a human who has seen the rise of civilization itself. She swam the Tigris and Euphrates, watched as Mesopotamia brought writing and the ziggurats into being and saw the flourishing of Babylon. She swam the Mediterranean and the Nile as the great pyramids were built and the Phoenicians sailed and the ancient Greeks constructed their temples and Alexandria shone its light across the sea and the Roman empire spread throughout the known world and Jesus walked the Holy Land. She swam the waters of the Indus as civilization grew and China rose and the Americas embraced the stars and the zero. She swam the coasts as Stonehenge and the mo'ai proclaimed their silhouette, as coral reefs began their dance of stone and redwoods greenwove the air in a lattice to the sun. She has read and learned more than any other soul in history. She is a great library of knowledge and of vast experience. And she told me of my change. She had just happened to spy me on the Sicilian shore on that fateful night. The light of the full moon glinting off my bottle of cognac. Smoke from my pipe dancing as phantoms in the gentle breeze. And she had desired to make another like herself. Call it selfishness, or loneliness, or boredom even, she could not be sure. She had created the other two elders as well. She knew of Blackbeard and was certain that I alone had created another. The other elders would not, as they saw any other as their sworn enemy. Even her. She avoids them, only to spare their most swift and assured death. I found it hard to hear—the details of my transformation—but was not upset with her. It was done and I had become what I had become and there she was. Another of my kind from whom I could learn so much and with whom I could perhaps find friendship. Even a deep and abiding kinship. I told her of my plan to eliminate the two elders and she did not dissuade me. It seemed that she may have even thought it to be a good idea, but had no desire for doing so herself. We talked of the possibility of creating others who could also share in a lasting friendship and in the Seven Seas. The possibility of creating a small community of our race. Of sharing the many thousands of years to come together instead of being apart, alone, isolated. It warmed my thoughts to speak of such. We will see what transpires. I have become quite cynical over the years. But I resolutely hope for the best. I would like such a community. A sense of belonging and comradeship would make being what I am so much more bearable. Regularly seeing others such as I would be a salve for my soul. Do I dare to hope? Yes. Yes, I dare to. I think that I shall permit myself this greatest and most meaningful of luxuries. Yes. I am resolved in the matter. I shall allow myself to hope once more.

I am a wereshark. This is my story.

About the Author

Justin T. O'Conor Sloane is an educator, writer, artist, editor, and publisher. He has been fascinated with science fiction and fantasy since a young lad and has been honored to publish some of the biggest names in the field. Justin's love of speculative fiction and SFF art inspired him to relaunch the classic science fiction magazines *Worlds of IF* and *Galaxy*, as well as originating various magazines, such as, *The Flying Saucer Poetry Review*, the first-ever literary journal devoted exclusively to art and literature about the UFO phenomenon—his poem about this subject, "The Third Law," was a finalist for the Science Fiction & Fantasy Poetry Association's Rhysling Award. Justin won the first Macmillan Education Onestopenglish international ELT poetry contest while teaching English at the Center for Interamerican Studies in Cuenca, Ecuador. He holds an MA in educational leadership with principal certification from The University of Texas Permian Basin and has been nominated for various teaching awards, including Humanities Texas. Justin is blessed with a wonderful and talented family and a dog that can sport a full mohawk from head to tail.